DOGS and

Volume 10

True Tales of the Old West

by

Charles L. Convis

PIONEER PRESS, CARSON CITY, NEVADA

Copyright © 1999 by Charles L. Convis
All Rights Reserved
Manufactured in the United States of America

Library of Congress Catalog Card Number: 96-68502

ISBN 1-892156-00-8 (Volume)
ISBN 0-9651954-0-6 (Series)

Printed by
KNI, Incorporated
Anaheim, California

CONTENTS

ILLUSTRATIONS

EXPLORER DOG

The twenty dollars Meriwether Lewis paid for the dog in Pittsburgh in 1803 was a lot of money, but the big black Newfoundland was a lot of dog. Lewis named him Scannon after Private George Shannon, youngest member of his detachment. Both the soldier and the dog would try anything and were afraid of nothing.

The soldiers moved down the Ohio River to Louisville and joined William Clark and the rest of the explorers. The men enjoyed shooting squirrels in trees along the river, and Scannon enjoyed jumping overboard to retrieve the game. The soldiers fried the squirrels, throwing choice morsels to the captain's new pet. Lewis described his dog as "active, strong and docile."

When the expedition reached the mouth of the Ohio and turned north, they met Shawnee Indians. The Indians, impressed with Scannon's size, offered Lewis three beaver skins. Lewis wrote in his journal: "I prized him much for his qualifications generally for the journey. Of course, there was no bargain."

After a boring winter in camp above St. Louis, Scannon was glad to be moving again. At first, he suffered from the heat. So he spent as much time in the water as he could — not hard to do as the expedition moved up the Missouri. Whenever possible, Scannon went out with the hunters. He helped catch deer and antelope all the way to the Mandan Villages. There the explorers spent their second winter. This time Scannon had Indian dogs to romp with, so he wasn't bored.

The travels west in 1805 were memorable for the dog, who had grown up in Pennsylvania. He hated the cockleburrs that stuck in his coat, but he loved retrieving geese. When they reached grizzly country, Scannon stayed in a constant state of alarm at night. His tireless barking kept the soldiers awake. Lewis and Clark finally told their men to flush the bears out of the thickets. They didn't care whether they killed the bears or just chased them away — anything to stop Scannon's barking and bring them nighttime peace.

The soldiers appreciated Scannon when they reached buffalo country. On the night of May 29, 1805, a large bull swam the Missouri, crossing to the side where the explorers had camped. Climbing out, the bull got tangled with a pirogue. In his panic, he ran straight for Lewis's tent. Scannon barked and growled until the buffalo veered away, and no one was hurt.

A few days later, Scannon jumped into the river to

retrieve a beaver that had been shot by a soldier. It was probably the first beaver he had ever seen. He learned it was not like a wounded squirrel. The beaver turned and bit Scannon severely. The dog almost bled to death from a severed artery. Lewis finally stopped the blood, and all the soldiers cheered.

As they met more Indians, the soldiers learned to eat dog meat, a delicacy with most tribes. But no one suggested eating Scannon. In fact, the soldiers shared rations with him. Considering Scannon's size, the rations must have equaled those issued to a soldier.

After another boring winter near the Pacific Ocean, Scannon bounded happily up the trail in spring, 1806. He howled in agony when mosquitos swarmed over him along the Columbia River.

Scannon was soon stolen by Chinook Indians. Private John Shields had stayed behind to buy himself a dog. The Chinooks accosted Shields, as he hurried to overtake the expedition. Shields drew his knife and drove the Indians away, but they sneaked up and stole Scannon, probably planning a gigantic feast.

When Lewis realized Scannon was gone, he ordered three men to chase the Indians. Up to that time, no one during their two years in Indian country had shot at an Indian. But Lewis told the soldiers to shoot if necessary to recover his dog. They chased the Indians a half mile before the thieves let the dog go. The soldiers returned triumphantly with Scannon.

On the divide between the Columbia and the Missouri, Private Reuben Fields shot a moose. The strange animal puzzled Scannon. He studied the odd-shaped antlers and sniffed at the huge body, as though to ask, "What in this strange world did you find this time?"

In fall 1806 Scannon was back in civilization. We have no mention of him after that. Three years later Meriwether Lewis either killed himself or was murdered near the Kentucky-Tennessee border. Perhaps his faithful dog was with him. Perhaps the courageous, fun-loving animal, who had become the mascot of the country's most important exploring expedition, spent the rest of his life roaming the woods, looking for more soldiers and their exciting adventures.

Suggested reading: Adrien Stoutenberg & Laura N. Baker, *Scannon, Dog with Lewis and Clark* (New York: Charles Scribner's Sons, 1959).

ABUSED DOG

We don't know the name; very likely he or she never had one. But it may have been the most abused dog in history.

The two men weren't bad men. William L. Sublette had trapped from Green River to Hudson's Bay. Now he was a proprietor, he and his partners, Jedediah Smith and David Jackson, having bought out William Ashley. The other man, Moses "Black" Harris, would become one of the half dozen most famous mountain men in history. Sublette selected him as his companion for the trip back to St. Louis to set up the 1827 fur-trade rendezvous. They wanted to be in St. Louis by March 1. They allowed two months for travel from their winter camp in Willow Valley, near present Cove, Utah.

The snow was too deep for horses, so Sublette and Harris got a pack dog from the Indians. On New Year's day they put on their snowshoes, strapped a fifty-pound pack of coffee, sugar and provisions on the dog, and started east in the mountain snow.

They struggled all the way to the Green River Valley without seeing any buffalo sign. They did see signs of Blackfoot Indians, and they kept away from the traveled ways as they approached South Pass. Everywhere they looked they saw a vast and frozen landscape, white and still as death. They melted snow for drinking water. On the 15th day they reached Independence Rock. Once in a while the men shot a bird or small animal, but the dog's pack of food got lighter much faster than they had planned.

They traveled down the Platte River, and wood became scarce. Some times they walked half the night to keep from freezing. At Ash Hollow, in present Nebraska, they saw Pawnee sign. Although they and the dog were all weak from hunger and it was easier to travel along the river, they veered away into the rougher highlands for three days. Then they saw sign of Omahas, a friendly tribe. They followed that trail and reached the Indian camp in four days.

The Omahas were hungry, too, and said they had no food for the mountain men. But Sublette traded his own knife, a trapper's most prized possession, for a dried buffalo tongue. He and Harris devoured the tongue on the spot. They ignored the dog. The pathetic animal was too weak to fight the Omahas' dogs for the food it needed.

As they traveled away from the Omahas, Sublette and

Harris noticed the dog's lameness. Every day it fell behind. Following the trail of its human companions, it would limp into camp long after dark.

When they reached Grand Island, Sublette was almost too weak to make his bed at night. He would scrape through the snow to the ground, wrap up in his blanket, and fall in an exhausted heap. Harris barely summoned enough strength to build a fire.

One night, as the dog approached their camp, Harris suggested that they kill and eat it. Sublette said he could never eat the faithful animal, no matter how hungry he got. But after more argument, he relented.

Harris picked up the axe and moved toward the dog, as the gaunt creature stared blankly into the fire. He hit the dog, and the stunned animal fell over and then struggled back to its feet. Harris swung again, but in his weakness, he missed. On the third blow, the axe head flew off and hit the dog. The wounded animal howled in pain and ran into the night.

Afraid the dog would escape, Sublette got out of his blanket and helped Harris search. They crawled on their hands and knees through the snow until they found where the wounded dog lay, bleeding and whimpering. Sublette wrapped his arms around the animal and held it while Harris stabbed his knife over and over into the dog's chest. Harris then threw the furry lump of bones on the fire.

Still the stubborn animal clung to life. It kicked convulsively until it escaped from the coals. The animal's piteous cries were more than Sublette could stand. He grabbed the axe, found strength he didn't know he had, and crushed the dog's skull.

Sublette wrapped himself back in his blanket while Harris roasted the dog. Harris scraped the scant flesh from the bones, divided it into two equal piles, and ate one. By morning, Sublette was able to choke down the pile set aside for him.

The food sustained the men for two more days. Then they shot a rabbit and came to an old trail of Kaw Indians. Now the going was easier. They killed four wild turkeys before they reached the Kaw camp, where they got more food. They reached St. Louis on March 4, just three days late.

Suggested reading: Dale L. Morgan, *Jedediah Smith and the Opening of the West* (Lincoln: Univ. of Neb. Press, 1971).

BILLY

David Douglas wanted a companion when he left England for the west coast of America in October, 1829. He chose Billy, a terrier from his native Scotland. Billy did not know that his new master was a world-famed exploring botanist, who would have one of North America's most important trees named for him. He soon learned, however, that his master had poor eyesight.

Billy was glad to get off the cramped ship after their seven-month voyage around Cape Horn to the Columbia River. Whenever the master stopped to inspect a plant or a leaf, Billy poked his nose under bushes, searching for small animals. He learned to wait while Douglas wrote in his notebook, peering closely at the page and moving his pencil slowly.

They met strange people who carried stick weapons and wore animal skins. Billy worried, but the master was unafraid. If the people pointed their stick weapons at him, the master raised his rifle and spoke harshly.

Billy worried most about the bears, which the master loved to hunt. Wild cattle, however, terrified the master. Billy liked to chase the cattle and bark at their heels, but the master always hurried away, his face drawn and pale from fear.

Billy never knew what the master's friend, down in the blue harbor country, had written about Douglas's fear of buffalo and wild cattle. The friend, Alfred Robinson, an early California historian, had said:

"Douglas would frequently go off, attended only by his little dog, and with rifle in hand search the wildest thicket in hopes of meeting a bear; yet the sight of a bullock grazing in an open field was to him more dreadful than all the terrors of the forest. He once told me that this was his only fear."

Billy began noticing that the master now had to turn his head to see. In fact Douglas was now totally blind in one eye. It was April 1833, and they had traveled to the far north. Douglas mentioned his "old terrier, a most faithful, and, to judge from his long grey beard, venerable friend. He has guarded me throughout all my journies."

That fall they sailed to the land of the islands. Billy did not like the high mountains, where the earth was warm and steam rose. The master could hardly see anything now. Many times he stumbled and fell. Billy would lick his face until he got up. Then he would search for what the master had tripped on, but the trails looked no harder than they ever had.

Billy was glad when they went to another island, where palm trees waved and women danced in grass skirts. But the master returned to the big island, saying something about meeting friends in Hilo, after they hiked across it one more time.

They stayed overnight at a cattle ranch and left early in the morning. They stopped for breakfast at a little hut by the trail. Billy, feeling his own age, wished the master would not travel so fast. The man in the hut walked a mile down the trail with them when they left.

Billy did not know that Ned Gurney made his living trapping wild cattle to sell to ranchers. Gurney warned Douglas about three pits on the trail ahead. One, carefully concealed, was right in the trail. The other two each held a steer, placed there to entice a wild bull to come near. The master slowed down as they approached the pits with the two steers. Then they saw the wild bull in the third pit.

Billy had no fear of wild cattle in the forest, but he cringed close to the master as they watched. The bull snorted and pawed dirt and lunged his horns into the sides of the pit. Billy shuddered. The master took off his backpack and moved closer. He cocked his head to one side, as he often did now to see.

Billy sensed a great danger. He did not know what to do. He whined and cried. Maybe he could grab the master's leg without hurting him and pull him back. Before he could act, the master's feet slipped, and he dropped from sight. Billy ran back to the pack and crouched on it. He heard screams and ugly thuds among the snorts and killing noises of the bull. He saw the master's body rise briefly above the edge of the pit. Then it disappeared again, and Billy could not bear to look.

Finally, the noises stopped. The bull breathed hard but was otherwise quiet. Billy closed his eyes and gripped the pack and did not let go. When the natives came up the trail, he was still there. The man at the hut came and killed the bull. They lifted the master out of the pit. Billy sniffed at what was left of him. He could tell it was the master by the smell; he could not tell by looking.

Suggested reading: John Davies, *Douglas of the Forests* Washington Press, 1980).

A PEPPERY BULLDOG

Each hide house at the San Diego harbor seemed to have about ten dogs that summer of 1843. Representing every color, size, and breed, their constant quarreling over well-picked bones produced much noise and confusion.

Three men from the *Barnstable* crew, a Lewey, a Tom, and Bill Thomes, took a fancy to a small bulldog that belonged to their hide house. He was clever and full of fight. But often a Mexican rode down to the beach accompanied by a cur twice as large as the little bulldog. The cur would clean out all the dogs, whether they belonged to Americans or Kanakas. The bulldog gave the larger dog a good fight, but he was always overpowered. Then the cur's owner would laugh and ridicule the Americans.

"Mucho bueno perro," he would taunt. "Can't you find something that will stand and fight and not turn tail like a cowardly gringo?"

Thomes and his friends had had enough! The honor of their country and their ship was at stake. They persuaded the bulldog's owner to sell him for a dollar. They fed the dog raw meat and kept him confined with light exercise. The ship's carpenter make a collar out of a tin plate. Two inches wide, it had sharp, scalloped edges and closed with a lock and key. They got a half pint of pepper sauce and a quarter pound of red pepper mixed with snuff from the steward.

One day, after they had the collar in place, they saw the Mexican riding down to the beach again, taunting his adversaries. The Americans rubbed the bulldog's hide full of pepper and snuff. The little animal, full of raw meat and tired of confinement, was ready to fight!

"Go get him, Jack," Thomes said.

When the surprised cur snapped down on Jack's neck, his teeth struck something harder than hair and skin. The captain of the *Barnstable* enjoyed watching the vindication of the Americans' honor, although he wondered why the Mexican cur sneezed so much in the short fight.

The cur fled and never came down to the beach again. The captain allowed Thomes to keep the bulldog on the ship. He made a good pet, although he never got over his love of fighting, no matter how large the foe.

Suggested reading: William H. Thomes, *On Land and Sea* (Boston: De Wolfe, Fiske and Company, 1884).

PRUNES

"You ever get lonely," asked Frank Hastings, early western cattleman, as he talked to Fred Reed one day. Reed had been knocking about the northwest for many years. He had punched cattle, and helped build the Northern Pacific Railroad.

"Lonely? I dodge it all I can, but sometimes you just can't avoid it." He looked off at the horizon, remembering. "The most terrible experience I ever had was when Prunes passed over."

Hastings kept silent, knowing a story was coming.

"He was a cayuse dog, an ugly brindle, a white-eyed cur. But I loved him and he loved me. I called him Prunes because I left him once to guard my camp while I went for more chuck, and he got into the prunes and ate them all up."

Hastings waited.

"Anyway, I was camped by the Snake River in Idaho, herding a bunch of cattle. It was a remote camp, and he was the only company I ever saw. Prunes ate with me, slept with me, and for five months was the only friend I had. I told him all my hopes and fears, my victories and defeats and failures. He'd wag his tail as much as to say, 'You're okay and I believe in you.'

"Well, anyhow, we was getting low on grub again and I decided one evening to go out and kill a jackrabbit. Prunes followed at my heels, wagging his tail at the prospects of something more exciting than watching a bunch of dumb cow brutes. I got my rabbit in about two hundred yards. It was coming on dark and Prunes was bouncing around in the sage. I decided to look for another rabbit, so he would have one, too. I saw what I though was another rabbit about forty feet away. I fired and heard the most godawful howls of pain from Prunes.

"He was done for. I lifted him into my arms and carried him back to the shack. I laid him down real careful like and sat beside him and cried like a baby. That night was the longest, most lonesome and dreary I ever spent. I dug his grave the next morning, but I couldn't stay there any longer. I loved him and he loved me. He trusted me and I had killed him. That was the worst thing that ever happened to me.

"I've been offered lots of fine dogs since, but I ain't never accepted one. I guess my heart is still out there in the sagebrush with Prunes."

Suggested reading: Frank S. Hastings, *A Ranchman's Recollections* (Chicago: The Breeder's Gazette, 1921).

DOGS FOR THE FAMILY

Not many dogs made it west with the emigrants. Oxen, horses, and mules could travel ten to fifteen miles, day after day, but not dogs. When soft feet got sore on hard, alkali trails, a sympathetic emigrant family could put a treasured pet in the wagon. But when all the children were afoot and family heirlooms were thrown out to lighten loads, dogs were left behind, too. Sioux, Cheyenne, and Shoshone Indians appreciated these additions to their pantries and hauling corps.

The Reed-Donner emigrant train, going west in 1846, was a notable exception. The wealthy James Reed family, traveling with the fanciest wagon ever seen on the trail, took their five dogs with them. Tyler, Barney, Trailer, Tracker and little Cash, the family pet, were welcomed into one of Reed's three wagons when they got tired and footsore.

Reed lost his best oxen in Wyoming. Then he lost the rest of them crossing the desert, west of Great Salt Lake. One by one, he abandoned his wagons. The family moved ahead on foot, using mules for packing and as mounts for wife Margaret, a near invalid, and baby Tommy. The dogs stayed with their family.

The season grew late and the nights turned cold. One night the Reeds bedded their four children down between two wagon sheets. James put the dogs on top to keep the children warm. He and Margaret sat up all night, their backs to the wind, to keep the dogs in place. After Virginia, 13, reached California, she wrote to her cousin, describing their journey. She said:

"It was the couldes night you most ever saw. The wind blew and if it haden bin for the dogs we would have Frosen."

Somewhere near present Winnemucca, Nevada, the Reeds were down to two mules, which Margaret and the smaller children rode. James had been banished from the company. He killed a man in self defense, but the company, resenting his former prosperity, ordered him out. The family dogs kept up with little trouble, especially after the mules died and Margaret and the children were all afoot.

The company could not cross the deep snow of the high mountains. They built rude shelters, killed the surviving oxen for food, and wondered who would be the first to starve.

The only other dog mentioned in the company was Towser, who belonged to Patrick Breen. Like the Reeds, the

Breens traveled with three wagons, two carrying supplies and one with beds for the children. Towser, also, was still with his family when the company made its camp at the lake.

By Christmas Tyler, Barney, Trailer and Tracker had all gone into the kettle to help feed the Reeds and the Graveses, with whom they shared their shelter. They still had Cash, the children's pet. The Reeds, having lost all their oxen, bought some from others, so they had a small supply of beef. But the beef was strips of thin flesh stripped from the bones of starved oxen. Without salt, it was a poor diet. The emigrants also ate the ox-hides and the hoofs and horns after they were softened in boiling water. The women boiled and re-boiled the ox-bones to get a thin soup. It differed some from plain water in flavor, but little in food value.

By early January the oxen Margaret Reed had bought from other emigrants had all been eaten. She and Virginia had captured and cooked a few field mice, but the family was starving, and it was time for a greater sacrifice. Virginia wrote in the letter to her cousin:

"We had to kill littel cash, the dog, and eat him. We ate his entrails and feet and hide and evry thing about him. O my dear cousin you dont now what trubel is."

Cash's small, emaciated body sustained the Reed family for a week. Eventually the entire family was rescued. It was the only family in the company which did not eat human flesh.

Patrick Breen put Towser in the kettle on February 24. All of that family, including seven children from 1 to 14, also survived.

Suggested reading: George R. Stewart, *Ordeal by Hunger* (Boston: Houghton Mifflin Company, 1960).

DEATH VALLEY DOG

Seven companies of 49'ers reached Salt Lake City too late to risk a northern crossing of the Sierras. The Donner tragedy, three years before, was much on everyone's mind. The emigrants elected to travel southwest, down the Old Spanish Trail to Los Angeles. When they reached Mountain Meadows in southwestern Utah, 107 of them, with their twenty-seven wagons, decided on a short cut. They headed west into the unknown mountains of southern Nevada. They had one dog with them. His name was Cuff. Their passage across what came to be called Death Valley is one of the epic journeys in American history. Cuff played his part.

When the four-month ordeal ended, four of the men lay dead in the desert and one had wandered away, his mind gone. But all the others, including four women and eleven children aged one to fourteen, came through safely.

Cuff, a hunting dog, good with deer, belonged to Asabel Bennett of Wisconsin. When Bennett put his wife, Sarah, and their three children into their California-bound wagon, Cuff went too. When the Bennetts reached the Missouri River, they joined with other emigrants traveling together to Salt Lake City.

While the Bennetts waited for the train to organize that would go down the Old Spanish Trail, William L. Manly walked by. Cuff was as happy as the Bennetts to see Manly, who had lived with them for a time. Manly and Cuff were old friends from hunting days in Wisconsin. Bennett invited Manly and Manly's friend, John Rogers, to travel with them to California.

The twenty-seven wagons turned out for the short cut in early November. Cuff had never seen such desolate country. The fact that he had walked all the way to Salt Lake City was remarkable. Most emigrants' dogs grew lame long before that and were abandoned on the trail. But the country Cuff now had to travel over was unlike anything he had ever seen. The emigrants went up one alkali canyon after another, searching for a way across the formidable mountains.

The water was even worse. Sometimes they went three days between seeps. The water, when found, tasted terrible, and sometimes neither Cuff nor the oxen nor the people could choke it down. By Christmas all organization had disappeared. The emigrants, now traveling in small individual groups, desperately fought to stay alive. Traveling with the

Bennetts were the Arcane family — two adults and two-year-old Charles — plus Manly and Rogers and the teamsters hired by both families.

In early February the group sent Manly and Rogers ahead to see if they could bring back food to the others, too weak to continue. They would wait by a spring, expecting their rescuers back in fifteen days.

Twenty-six days later, Manly and Rogers returned with a pack of food on a little, one-eyed mule. The others had already given up hope. When Manly said they had started back with three horses and more food, but the horses had perished, the despair deepened. All the time Manly and Rogers were gone, the weakened emigrants had been eating their oxen, scraping a little meat from the bones and cooking the blood.

Manly finally persuaded his friends to get on their feet and try to walk out. They would use the remaining oxen for food on the trail. The women and children were allowed to ride the stronger oxen.

The starving emigrants only had strength to carry the clothing on their backs. Mrs. Arcane decided to wear her fanciest dress and bonnet. She put on a long dress and beribboned bonnet, and the men hoisted her to the back of an ox. The frightened animal summoned enough strength to run and buck in an attempt to throw her off. The others, too weak to stand firmly, lay on the ground and laughed while Cuff barked at the spectacle. The laugh seemed to help. One by one, the people got to their feet and started toward Los Angeles.

Manly said the dog proved as tough as the rest of them. They found a bag of wheat which Manly and Rogers had cached when their horses died. They had to kill an ox every two or three days for more food. They even softened the hooves and horns in the fire and ate them. One man could carry the meat from an entire ox on his back.

But all of them, including Cuff, reached safety at the San Fernando Mission. After the people had recovered their strength, Bennett and Manly went north to prospect. Manly wrote that the faithful dog was "lost, strayed, or stole" while they mined at Georgetown.

We hear no more about the Death Valley Dog.

Suggested reading: William L. Manly, *Death Valley in '49* (Los Angeles: Borden Publishing Co., 1949).

SAN FRANCISCO PAIR

The daily promenade on Montgomery Street was an important part of life in gold rush San Francisco. Key participants were the Timeless One, immaculately dressed in his frock coat, the Great Unknown, a mysterious old man with fine military bearing and the elastic step of youth, Topsy-Turvy, her hat upside down and her coat inside out, and Emperor Norton, insane but always greeted with the respect due royalty. Bringing up the rear would be two mongrel dogs, Bummer and Lazarus.

Bummer showed up first. Homeless, he was supposed to have been born on the prairies while his mother traveled to California in a wagon train. A scrappy puppy fighting Indians, he lost his master and reached Sacramento a disappointed and disgusted dog. He was not happy until he reached San Francisco. Now that was the city for him!

Bummer got his name from cursing waiters in the places he entered. But the short-legged, black and white shaggy mongrel, described as bulldog in his fighting quarters and Newfoundland in his vital parts, caught on fast. He learned to wait at the entrance of a restaurant or saloon until a large party walked in. He would nonchalantly follow, showing by poise and manners that he was with friends to whom he belonged. Each man, thinking Bummer was a friend of someone else in the group, would slip scraps to him. He never begged or acted hungry. His regal manner showed a confidence that his "master" would take proper care. Bummer got his sustenance the same way Emperor Norton did, by imperial demand.

Bummer was soon acquainted with every restaurant on his beat, and he had his favorites for breakfast, lunch and dinner. He preferred to cruise the east side of Montgomery Street. He never took anything extra for a rainy day. He relied on a generous and abundant providence to provide for each day as it came.

Bummer's notoriety grew in 1861. An excavation in the street revealed a small army of hated rats. Bummer jumped into the hole and killed so many so fast the crowd marveled. Then people tried to outdo each other, feeding Bummer. He took it all in stride as though he deserved it.

One day, filled with food and satisfied with life, Bummer stood on the walk in front of a saloon watching a large dog attack an emaciated, mangy dog, yellowish-black in color, a cross between a cur and a hound, with a dash of terrier. Bummer leaped into the fray and sent the attacker yelping down the street. The piteous victim, one leg almost bitten off, limped away behind his savior. At first Bummer treated the bedraggled cripple with contempt mixed with pity. But that night the dogs were seen sleeping in a doorway. The cripple had the inner berth. Bummer was trying to keep the mutt warm.

The next day, for the first time in memory, Bummer was seen carrying off bits of meat from his eating establishments. Town sports followed him to a vacant lot. They found the other dog under a pile of empty boxes. Bummer was dropping morsels to him, coaxing him to eat. In a few days, the cur followed Bummer as he made his daily rounds. The sports christened the dog Lazarus, since he had been raised from the dead by the power and love of Bummer.

The Board of Supervisors passed an ordinance that all unmuzzled dogs on the street were to be impounded and then shot if not claimed within twenty-four hours. An indignant citizenry presented a long petition to the Board, asking for relief for Bummer and Lazarus. Another ordinance was passed, giving the two dogs permission to roam the streets, unmuzzled and unmolested. By law they had become permanent guests of the city.

As the two dogs worked the streets together, they displayed cooperation and unselfishness that would draw human envy. Bummer always led in a fight, while Lazarus lay back, encouraging his friend and protector. Bummer did the biting, Lazarus the barking.

One Saturday night Bummer was accidentally locked up in a news depot. Lazarus, inconsolable, hunted high and low all day Sunday. He refused food. He even skipped his usual breakfast at Chase's on Monday to continue searching for his friend. Then he heard a scratching on a window when he passed Bummer's temporary prison. Lazarus dove through the glass, smashing it to pieces. He stayed inside with his friend until the door was opened and they could walk outside together to freedom.

The dogs took on the role of city rat killers. Once, with the help of club-wielding men, they killed four hundred in two hours. Another time, without help, they killed eighty-five in twenty minutes. Their fame spread.

Lazarus died first. He was run over by a fire engine in

October, 1863. The whole town took part in the public funeral. His skin was stuffed and put on display in one of Bummer's favorite saloons.

But Bummer mourned. He lost all appetite for life. He lost his self respect, grew careless in his personal appearance, and slunk away to obscurity.

In September, 1865, a drunk kicked Bummer down a stair, injuring him seriously. The drunk was fined a hundred dollars and sent to jail when he could not pay. His cellmate, sharing San Francisco's affection for the dog he had kicked, "popped him on the smeller."

The whole town realized that they still loved the dog, even though they had seen little of him for many months. Citizens avidly followed daily newspaper reports on Bummer's condition.

Bummer died on November second. Many reporters wrote mournful tidings. Mark Twain's obituary in the Virginia City *Territorial Enterprise* was the most philosophical:

"The old vagrant, Bummer, is really dead at last, and although he was always more respected than his obsequious vassal, the dog Lazarus, his exit has not made half as much stir in the newspaper world as signalized the departure of the latter. I think it is because he died a natural death, died with friends around him to smooth his pillow and wipe the death damps from his brow and receive his last words of love and resignation; because he died full of years and honor and disease and fleas. Lazarus died with his boots on, so his shortcomings were excused and his virtues heralded to the world."

Suggested reading: Pauline Jackson, *City of the Golden Fifties* (Berkeley: University of Calif. Press, 1941).

BUFFALO FIGHTER

The Fourth Cavalry, stationed at Fort Concho in West Texas, enjoyed hunting at their remote outpost. The many cur dogs that hung around the post would follow the soldiers into the field to hunt wolves, coyotes, jackrabbits, and antelopes. King, a white English bulldog taken over by the regimental band, was one of the hunt leaders. He had learned to pull down beeves at the fort's slaughter corral. Then Colonel Ranald Mackenzie took command in February, 1871, and the recreational hunts ended.

"We're here to fight Indians," he said.

In March he led five companies to Fort Richardson to garrison that post. King and the regimental band were part of the detachment.

On March 31 the soldiers dropped from the high mesa into vast buffalo herds on the plains below. The buffaloes crowded against the troopers and their wagon train of supplies. Nervous troopers began firing.

"Stop firing," the officers ordered.

A gigantic bull, the herd leader, had been wounded, as the animals rumbled along in front of the barking dogs. King ran up, sprang to the bull's throat, locked his jaws, and the battle began. The troopers watched in awed silence as the bull whirled King in great circles. Although they had never seen King let go in a fight, the troopers thought he had no chance in this unequal struggle. Every minute they expected the courageous dog to be dashed to the ground and crushed to death.

The bull dropped to his knees, trying to gore his foe. He regained his feet in rage and swung and snapped King like a rag doll. Bloody foam flecked the bull's long beard. His eyes flashed fire. King, white when the battle started, gradually turned red from the spraying blood of his adversary. King's brute instincts and his tenacity and training led him to hold on as he was flung back and forth like a popping whip.

The bull gradually weakened as King, growing redder and dirtier, lost all semblance of his former self. Then two troopers stepped forward and fired their carbines into the beast's heart. The bull fell to the earth. Not until then did King let go.

A few months later an order was issued to kill all cur dogs at Fort Concho. A special order exempted King.

Suggested reading: R. G. Carter, "Buffalo Vs. Bulldog" in *Outing* (New York, October, 1887).

SLEEP ON, OLD FELLOW

In September, 1879, Major Tom Thornburgh led a combined force from Forts Steele and D. A. Russell in Wyoming Territory to the White River Indian Agency in Colorado to protect it from rampaging Utes. Thornburgh and most of his command were killed. Colonel Wesley Merritt led another force from the forts to rescue survivors, if any could be found.

When Merritt's men neared the agency they came upon a freight wagon that had been following Thornburgh's command. The teamster, his helper, and their dog had been killed, the wagon burned, and the mules stolen. Merritt's men hurried on, afraid of what they would find ahead.

The relief command rescued the few survivors and started back to their posts. On the way they passed the burned wagon again. This time they saw a tiny puppy whimpering at the side of its dead mother. One of the soldiers picked up the puppy, stroked its soft fur, and carefully stowed him with his gear.

We don't know whether the puppy was raised by an infantryman at Fort Steele or a cavalryman at Fort Russell. We do know that the soldiers named the puppy Thornburgh in honor of the major. Thornburgh grew up with a deadly hatred of Indians and sneak attackers. The latter hatred first brought Thornburgh into the limelight.

One dark night a soldier on guard duty heard the sounds of a terrible fight. The corporal of the guard brought a light, and the soldiers saw Thornburgh astride a prostrate, unconscious man. A sack nearby with its contents strewn about told the story.

The man had robbed the commissary, and Thornburgh saw him sneaking away in the darkness. The thief barely recovered from the wounds inflicted by the dog's sharp fangs.

Up to this time Thornburgh had been treated as just another cur on the post, subject to being shot if found on the parade ground. The post commander visited the dog the next morning. Thornburgh, sore, bloody and bruised, could hardly stand. His worst wound was a deep knife cut running down his side.

"Call the post veterinarian," the commander ordered. "Tell him to do everything he can." He reached down and patted Thornburgh's head. "And the order about shooting

THORNBURGH AND FRIENDS
(Buck Buchanan wearing stovepipe hat)
Wyoming Division of Cultural Resources

dogs found on the parade ground no longer applies to this fellow."

When Thornburgh recovered his health, the soldiers gave him a new collar with a brass tag containing his name. He also had a new hatred. He remembered the flash of the knife in the near darkness before it ripped his side open. From then on, he was ready to attack when he saw a knife raised or drawn.

Thornburgh remained a hero to the soldiers. One night, on an Indian campaign, he warned the sentinel that Indians were sneaking up to capture horses. The warning saved the horses and probably some lives.

Thornburgh eventually showed up at Fort Bridger in southwestern Wyoming. There a civilian teamster, Buck Buchanan, befriended the dog. Before this Thornburgh had been friendly with soldiers and treated most civilians with contempt. But Buck's patience finally won him over, and the two became inseparable.

Thornburgh's devotion to Buck became a jealous one. He would allow other men to shake hands with his master, but that was all. If they tried to slap Buck on the back or get too familiar, Thornburgh was ready to fight.

One night two drunken soldiers got into a fight. One of them drew a knife and raised his arm to stab the other. As the arm came down and the knife flashed, Thornburgh leaped through the air, grabbing the arm in his teeth. The assailant was thrown to the ground and the knife went flying into the air. The man Thornburgh attacked became his friend because the dog had kept him from killing one of his comrades.

Thornburgh also saved the life of a small boy who had fallen into a raging river. The boy's grateful parents presented the dog with a new collar. On it was a silver plate engraved: For Most Distinguished Gallantry.

On September 27, 1888, at Fort Bridger, Buck got orders to hitch up his mule team and report for a hauling job. He went to the corral and sent Thornburgh in to bring the team out. The dog had done this many times, and he enjoyed the assignment. This time, however, a large number of unbroken mules in the corral made all the animals nervous, and Thornburgh was unable to get the right ones to the gate. Buck saw his difficulty and, fearing for the dog, called him back.

Thornburgh either couldn't hear or was unwilling to give up on his task. He got one of the mules headed for the gate, but an unbroken mule kicked at him viciously. The dog slipped as he tried to swerve out of the way, and the hooves pounded squarely against his side. He was hurled several feet through the air. He lay motionless in the corral.

Buck rushed in, picked up the unconscious dog, and carried him to his own bunk. He laid Thornburgh down gently and stared through wet eyes at his faithful friend. He patted the dog's neck, remembering many things which he had seen and more which he had heard others tell.

Thornburgh never recovered.

Few people know where Major Thornburgh was buried, and apparently none know now where Buck rests. But every visitor to Fort Bridger state park can see the grave of Thornburgh, the heroic dog. His granite marker says: Man never had a better, truer, braver friend. Sleep on, Old Fellow. We'll meet across the range.

Suggested reading: Albert C. Allen, *Thornburgh* (No publisher - Wyoming State Museum? - no date).

BOB-TAILED HITCH HIKER

When twelve-year-old Jack Graves saw the puppy, he wanted him more than anything. During the seven years the family had been in California, ranching near Marysville, Jack had grown to love dogs and horses. If he could talk the Sacramento horse racer out of it, it would not be his first dog, just the best.

It was the ugliest thing Jack had ever seen. Born to a half-mastiff mother and an unknown father, it had a natural bob tail. The most distinguishing marks were the eyes. Dropping away from the nose at an angle, they were covered with the loose folds of excess skin that enclosed the little body.

But the owner said "no" to Jack's entreaty. "I expect to get at least fifty dollars for that one."

It was 1864 and the Graves family were in Quincy on their annual trek to visit Uncle Jimmy and see the horse races. Jack, penniless, knew another racer, Mart Gibson, who might help. He had been exercising horses for Mart and had even filled in as a jockey when Mart's regular jockey, an Indian boy, was thrown from his horse and killed.

"Nobody will pay for that puppy," Jack told Mart. "He's so ugly he's pretty. See if you can get him to give him to me."

"I'll do what I can."

The day before the Graves family were to start the two-day wagon ride back to their ranch, Mart took Jack aside.

"He gave me that pup, and I'll give him to you. But we can't let anybody know."

Jack jumped up and down, his eyes gleaming.

"So you meet me at the Quincy Hotel at four in the morning. I'll have the pup in a sack. You can start down the trail and let your family catch up. Then the guy'll never know that I gave him to you."

Jack and Mart were the only people awake in Quincy the next morning when the happy boy shouldered the wiggling bag, the puppy's head sticking out a hole. Jack walked along cheerfully for a mile or two. Then he laid the twenty-pound load down for a rest. After eating a biscuit and getting a drink from a stream near the road, he remembered how the puppy had enjoyed chasing him during the many visits he had made to pet the animal.

So Jack shook the puppy out of the bag, patted his head, and entreated him to follow as Jack ran on ahead. The puppy sat back on his haunches and howled. The long, dismal howl would have embarrassed a wolf. Jack was afraid the whole country would know what he had, so he stuffed the hitch hiker back into the sack and trudged on.

The sun climbed higher. Jack's shirt was soaked with sweat. But no matter how he tried, he could not get the puppy to follow. Stubborn, he was content to bounce along on Jack's back, his head sticking out the hole, as he contemplated the passing Feather River valley.

When Jack heard the wagon coming up behind, he sat down, expecting his mother. It was a fruit peddler, but he gave Jack a ride to Spanish Ranch. The hotel there fed Jack breakfast and gave the puppy milk. Then Jack sat in a chair on the porch with the happy puppy curled up in his lap, waiting for his family to catch up.

After a while Jack heard a wagon approaching from the west. It was the Sacramento man who had given the puppy to Mart! He spoke pleasantly to Jack until he saw the puppy. Then, accusing Jack of stealing the animal, he grabbed it and put it in his buggy. His wife protested against taking the puppy away from Jack.

"He stole him from Mart Gibson," the man said. "I'm taking him back."

But the dog rescued Jack. He sat back on his haunches and howled and howled. After the whole population of Spanish Ranch had gathered round in curiosity and awe, the man relented. He picked the puppy up by the loose folds of his neck and handed him back to Jack.

"Take him, you little thief," he said. "I hope he brings you bad luck."

Jack noticed a merry twinkle in the wife's eyes as they drove away. Jack's mother and brother caught up with him and the new addition to the family. Jack called him Tige after the first dog he had owned.

Tige grew huge and powerful. By the time he was two, he had whipped every dog that would fight within ten miles of the Graves ranch. He could throw a large steer with ease. He even fought wild hogs in the river bottoms. With Tige's help Jack hunted those acorn-fattened hogs every fall.

Tige was a great watchdog, but one morning they found him dead in the yard, poisoned. A short time later thieves raided their smokehouse, stealing all the meat which Tige had helped them kill.

Suggested reading: Jackson A. Graves, *California Memories* (Los Angeles: Times-Mirror Press, 1930).

CANINE CALLIOPE

Like thousands of his countrymen, Smith Hurles came to America during the Irish potato famine. He stopped in Boston long enough to marry and have four children. But the gold fields beckoned, and in 1857 he moved to California, stopping at Oroville on the Feather River.

Besides his family Smith brought his battered accordion and a heart full of music. But Oroville, the roughest mining town in northern California, was no place to raise a family. So Smith moved six miles east to a beautiful meadow bordered by stately oaks. He built a hotel to provide food and music to miners, gamblers, working girls, and others passing through. He called it Boston Ranch.

As his children grew, Smith taught them to play the piano and fiddle and to sing old Irish ballads. One day a large ragged hound of diverse ancestry showed up, looked around, and decided Boston Ranch was the place for him. Smith called him Old Dan, and taught him to lift his grizzled muzzle to the sky and wail as the children played their instruments. Miners, who found humor where others seldom looked, loved it.

When Smith had taught his children everything he knew about music, he turned his attention to the eager, four-legged student. Night after night the old dog would stretch and strain to reach higher and higher notes, matching the wonderful melodies that poured from Smith's accordion.

Old Dan's howls flowed across the meadows and into the hills. On crisp autumn nights with a full moon the coyotes even hushed their customary serenade, as though ashamed to mix their puny voices with such a master.

A new game developed in the Feather River country as Old Dan's fame spread from mining camp to mining camp. Men brought musical instruments to Boston Ranch to test the dog's powers. Bets were made on Old Dan's ability to out-howl his mechanical competition. The dog's backers never lost. The louder the music, the louder his response. The dog's reputation reached into all the camps of the northern Sierra.

One day a traveling organ grinder came by. As he played for handouts in the streets and saloons of Oroville, a high-rolling gambler took him aside. After assuring himself of the organ's range, the gambler hired the grinder to play only for him.

"You only play when I say," he cautioned.

"You pay mister, you call the tune."

The gambler rode out to Boston Ranch with the challenge. The duel was set, and Smith placed a large bet on Old Dan.

Word spread quickly. A large crowd of miners gathered. Smith's saloon was busy as the gambler covered all bets. The organ grinder sat alone in a corner, nursing a bottle of whiskey and waiting for the word to begin.

Finally Smith said it was time for the contest. The crowd rushed outside. Smith played a few chords to warm his old dog up. Then he nodded his head, and the gambler signaled his man to start.

The organ's first notes were as soft as an aspen whisper in a summer breeze. Dan cocked an ear but made no reply. As the organ played louder, Dan raised his graying muzzle and the first soft whines welled up from his old throat.

Then the grinder bent to his task. Faster and faster he turned the handle. Mournful plaints rose from the box as if trying to leap over the foothills to the high mountains beyond. But Old Dan matched his foe, screech for screech. The air filled with wails. Some of the crowd held hands to their ears.

The battle grew in volume, and Old Dan's backers added their cheers of support. Feeding on their enthusiasm, the dog reached higher and higher, twisting his head from side to side, his eyes partially closed.

The meadow had become a huge reservoir of noise. Birds lifted themselves into the air and fled to quieter skies. Dan's nose rose higher and higher as he strained to meet the challenge. He reached a pitch he had never heard before. His throat muscles rolled and writhed like convulsing snakes, and his eyes closed in the throes of super-dog effort.

Then Old Dan stopped. He lowered his head, looked Smith lovingly in the eye as though remembering their many nights of practice. Dan toppled over, his chest heaved, the organ stopped, and the crowd hushed in wonderment. The dog whimpered softly and lay still. Old Dan was dead.

Smith picked up his hound, cradled him gently in his arms, and walked toward a grove of oaks, tears flushing his eyes. The crowd paid off the gambler and returned to the saloon to toast the memory of Old Dan.

The faithful hound's heart could not quite match his devotion to the master and the master's music.

Suggested reading: Bill Talbitzer, *The Days of Old, The Days of Gold* (Oroville: Las Plumas Publ. 1973).

SULTAN ON WATCH

Old Jim Bridger, most famous guide in the early West, was slow to die. The army paid him off in 1867, and he went home to his Missouri farm. At sixty-three he was already a legend, but the army had younger scouts. Shrunk by age, he still stood tall and slender, but his small, gray eyes were not as piercing as in his youth.

"I wish I war back in the mountains agin," he would say. "A man kin see so much farther in that country."

So the old man would sit on the porch, his face and his thoughts turned west. Faithful Sultan waited at his side. Bridger's daughter, Virginia, had got him the dog, along with Ruff, a gentle old horse.

Jim liked Sultan and Sultan knew it. Of course, Ruff was alright, too, but horses were to use, not to like. Jim would reach his hand down as he rocked. Sultan's warm head and moist tongue always felt good. The dog would wait patiently, knowing that Virginia would saddle Ruff and bring him around for the morning ride before the sun got too high.

Jim thought of his three Indian wives — first the Flathead, then the Ute, finally the Shoshoni. All good women, but the Ute's daughter, Virginia, was such a comfort to her old father. Virginia's mother had died in childbirth, and Jim raised the baby on buffalo milk.

Jim loved to travel over his 640-acre farm, which is now a suburb of Kansas City. At first the old man could shuffle along with a cane, in spite of an old rupture. A happy Sultan would bound alongside.

Jim enjoyed walking through the hickory and hackberry trees in the creek bottom. The sound of the stream rushing along the rocky bottom brought back memories of beaver lodges in Rocky Mountain willow banks.

Jim liked to inspect his apple orchard. He was proud of the apples, and every fall he sent basketsfull, along with fresh cider, to his neighbors.

During the summer he loved to go to his wheat field to see how it was growing. When Jim's eyesight suddenly turned worse, he would get down on hands and knees and brush the wheat leaves across his face to learn when the crop was beginning to head out. As his eyesight disappeared, he relied more and more on Ruff to get him around. Sultan still followed, glad for the daily excursions with his master.

By 1875, Jim was completely blind. He could still ride

Ruff to the places on the farm he wanted to visit. His skill at not getting lost had been legendary on the plains and in the mountains. In those days, if he saw a ridge or a valley or a lake or a river, he could always remember how to get back to it again. He could even tell what it would look like, approaching from the opposite side. This uncanny sense of direction, learned in hostile Indian country when his life was in the balance, served him well on his farm.

Jim Bridger never could read or write. But he could make a map of every place he had ever been, from the British possessions to New Mexico and west to the Pacific Ocean.

But now there was a difference. Sometimes Ruff would end up in a corner or a thicket, and Jim could not get him out. No matter how Jim pulled the reins, Ruff would either stand still or turn around and around in his tracks. Sitting on a horse when you were completely blind and over seventy years old was not like walking through strange mountains as a young man, all senses alert for danger. When Jim couldn't get Ruff to move, he would call out to his dependable dog:

"Sultan, run on and tell Verginny where we are. I cain't git this damn horse to do nothin' right."

Then Sultan would run to the house, find Virginia, and bark and whine until she put down her work.

"Alright, Sultan, show me where he is this time." Then Sultan would bound away, looking back to make sure she followed. When they reached the master, Virginia would lead Ruff home with Sultan following, content that he had again discharged his duty.

With Sultan's help, Jim Bridger stayed active until he died at seventy-seven. He suffered from rheumatism, goiter, and an old rupture, but never from boredom.

Suggested reading: J. Cecil Alter, *James Bridger, Trapper, Frontiersman, Scout and Guide* (Columbus, Long's College Book Co., 1951).

ANTELOPE HUNTER

Dodge City, Kansas, was in the middle of great game country. The first permanent settlers, following buffalo hunters, kept packs of greyhounds. The man with the best and largest pack got his nickname from his love of the sport. He was the town mayor, James H. "Dog" Kelly.

The first winter of Dodge City's existence was one of deep snow. By late November, 1872, the antelope had moved in from the hills to bunch up by the thousands in the river bottoms.

The morning after a great snowstorm in December, which killed about a hundred buffalo hunters, Kelly took his pack of hounds and several sportsman friends out for a hunt. A half mile west of town they struck a large band of antelope, and the dogs soon caught all the animals the men could carry. Not wanting to kill for useless slaughter, Kelly called in the hounds and they all went home.

Kelly's favorite hound was a six months old pup, Jim. He was big boned, well muscled, and very large for his age. When the hunting party got back to town, Jim was missing! Kelly put the other hounds away and struck out, looking for Jim.

A mile or two from where they had quit the hunt, Kelly found a dead antelope. A few miles further he found another. The trail of dead antelopes — about a dozen of them — continued until Kelly reached Nine-Mile Ridge, twenty miles west of Dodge City. There he found Jim, exhausted, lying beside his last kill.

Jim's trail of dead antelopes showed that the frightened animals had followed along the Arkansas River, where the wind had swept the snow to shallower depths. Kelly carried Jim home in front of his saddle. No amount of money could buy the dog after that hunt!

In later years, as Jim aged, he would sometimes be on a hunt twenty or thirty miles away from Dodge City. Then the men and the other dogs would quit and return home. Jim would stagger in three or four days later, all tired out. Several days would pass before he noticed anything but food or water. Kelly's friends would then kid him by saying, "Looks like old Jim has quit hunting."

"Not until the antelopes quit," Kelly would reply.

Suggested reading: Robert M. Wright, *Dodge City: The Cowboy Capital and the Great Southwest* (ca 1913).

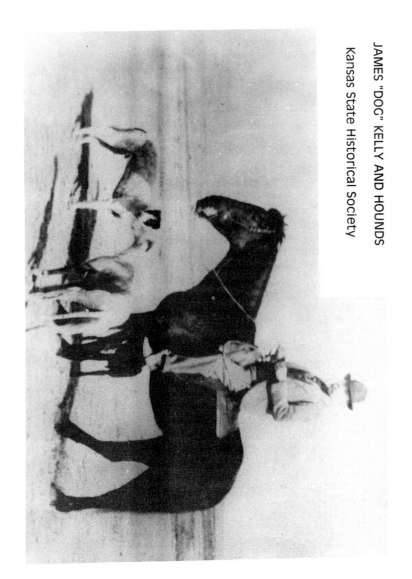

JAMES "DOC" KELLY AND HOUNDS

Kansas State Historical Society

THE UNTIRING

Captain William F. Butler's closest companion on his 4000-mile exploration of Western Canada in 1872-73 was Cerf Vola, his 100-pound Husky sled dog. Butler had used the dog two years before on the Red River Expedition against the rebellious Metis. Glad to find the dog again, he made him fore-goer, leader of the team. Cerf Vola was clean limbed, long wooled, and deep chested. His ears pointed forward, and his tail curled closely over his broad back.

To bring his team up to strength, Butler bought Major, another large Husky. Both Major and Cerf Vola came from Lame Deer Lake, and Butler wondered if they were related. Their resemblance caused a horrible mistake as Butler's Indian helpers hooked the team up one morning in pre-dawn darkness. They put Major in the lead and Cerf Vola next to the sled. When Butler realized the mistake, he switched the dogs, but Cerf Vola picked on Major unmercifully from then on. Major gave out a few weeks later and had to be replaced.

Butler described Cerf Vola as a tactful dog. He never fought a pitched battle. As soon as they entered a strange Hudson's Bay Company fort, Cerf Vola would take charge of all the company's dogs. Butler marveled at his dog's mysterious power over other dogs. Cerf Vola would bound a step or two toward two or three large dogs with an expression that seemed to say, "Somebody hold me back so I don't destroy these lowly curs." The strange dogs would run, and Cerf Vola would be in command of yet another fort. Within a few minutes he would know exactly where the company stored its whitefish, its pemmican, and its dried meat.

Butler traveled from Fort Garry to the forks of the Saskatchewan in fall 1872. Then he waited until early February, giving the rivers time to freeze solid so he could follow the ice road to the west side of the Rocky Mountains. Many dogs, horses, and full and half blood Indians traveled with him. But only Cerf Vola stayed with him every step of the 4000-mile journey. One time he wrote that he was traveling alone over a section of the trail, with only Cerf Vola for company. In fact, he had three Indians with him at the time, but he never considered them equal to the dog as companions.

Butler repeatedly referred to his dog as The Untiring. A normal day's travel with a 200-pound load on the sled was thirty-five or forty miles. But his longest day's travel — fifty-six miles — was made with only Cerf Vola and one other dog in harness. The dogs seemed to sense the importance of getting on to the next major stop, Fort Chipewyan at the west end of Lake Athabaska.

Butler mentioned that sometimes Cerf Vola got lame. Then he would look around to see if Butler was going to put boots on him. Whether Butler did or not, the dog would throw his weight back into the harness, put his head down, and trudge forward again without complaint.

Butler followed the Peace River from Fort Chipewyan through the Rocky Mountains. There he switched to horses and a canoe, taking only Cerf Vola and what Indian guides he could pick up for the journey down the Fraser River to the Pacific. Even without a sled, and whether they rode or marched on foot, Cerf Vola led the way. But he got a rude surprise when they entered Fort St. James. This was the first Hudson's Bay Company fort he had ever entered without pulling a sled in. As soon as they were inside, four large hauling dogs pounced on him. Butler rescued the dog before he was badly beaten, but Cerf Vola spent the rest of the day in seclusion under Butler's bed. Apparently his role as the fore-goer on a sled team had much to do with his earlier prestige. Without that, he was just another visiting dog, subject to attack by the local sled dogs.

At the end of the long journey, Butler disposed of his last horses and paid off the last Indian guides. With Cerf Vola as his only companion, he traveled through Oregon and on to Mount Shasta, San Francisco, and Yosemite. Then he took a train to New York.

Butler, a captain in the British Army, had to bid his old friend a sad goodbye in New York. Butler was joining his regiment in Africa, a place wholly unsuitable for a Husky sled dog. He did mention that Cerf Vola took civilized life in the United States in stride except for two things. He could never get used to butcher shops or brass bands. He thought the meat hung in the shops for his benefit. He fled in fear from the noisy bands. Butler remembered the dog fondly for the rest of his life.

Suggested reading: William F. Butler, *The Wild North Land* (Edmonton: M. G. Hurtig, Ltd., 1968).

PROUD MOTHER

Several dogs lived in Adobe Walls when the Indians attacked that morning of June 27, 1874. One of them, a big Newfoundland, was owned by the freighting Shadler brothers. The mysterious sound of a ridge beam cracking in Hanrahan's Saloon had most of the trading post's people awake in time to resist the attack. But nothing warned the Shadler brothers or their dog.

The brothers were killed and scalped as they slept in their wagon. So was their dog. He was scalped by slicing away a patch of fur from his side.

The rest of the dogs, including Billy Dixon's Fannie, ran and hid in the timber. Dixon carried word of the attack to Dodge City. When Nelson Miles led his troopers into Fort Dodge about August 1, he hired Dixon as scout to lead his troops to the besieged buffalo-hunting outpost.

The Indians were gone when the troopers reached Adobe Walls. Miles continued the patrol, with Dixon scouting in the lead. They returned to Adobe Walls in early October.

Shortly after they arrived, Dixon was thrilled to see Fannie come into the post. She was a "highly intelligent" setter. Hearing nothing about her since the dogs had run into the timber, Dixon could only assume that she had been killed by Indians or had starved to death.

After Dixon petted and fed Fannie, she ran off again. But she soon returned, this time with something in her mouth. She wagged her tail for attention, and the onlookers grinned, as happy as small boys, at what she had. She dropped a fat, bright-eyed little puppy gently on to a pile of bedding. Then she frisked about in pure delight as Dixon and the others grinned.

While the men fussed over who could next hold the puppy, Fannie bounded away again. She returned with another puppy, placing it gently beside the first one. Two more trips brought the family up to four wriggling, happy puppies. There was no question from their appearance that the father was the big Newfoundland, owned by the Shadlers and killed in the attack.

When Miles' command pulled out, a contented Fannie and her babies were given a snug place in the mess wagon.

Suggested reading: Olive K. Dixon, *Life of "Billy" Dixon* (Dallas: P. L. Turner Company, 1927).

SHEPHERD

When the Casner brothers sold their California gold mine, they filled leather bags with twenty-dollar gold coins, and invested part of their money in a flock of sheep. They hired a young Navajo boy and herded their flock east, looking for free land in the Texas Panhandle.

Word of their riches and intentions preceded them. When they reached the Canadian River in summer 1876 and started to graze their flock, Sostenes l'Archevêque, the most violent and hated man in New Mexico, rode up to their sheep camp.

He shot one brother down in cold blood after learning that the other brother and the Indian boy were bringing the flock in from the grazing grounds. He hid until the other brother approached, and shot him down. Then he rode out to meet the Indian boy.

Sostenes's questions about the gold made the boy suspicious. The dogs began snarling. The outlaw shoved his gun into the boy's stomach.

"Tell me where the gold is hidden," he demanded.

One dog leaped at Sostenes, throwing him off balance. He whirled and shot the animal in the head. A final demand brought information about one bag of gold. The boy claimed to know nothing about others.

Sostenes clubbed the boy to death with his pistol. While he was doing that, the second dog attacked. The outlaw interrupted his gory work long enough to kill that dog.

After finding the bag of gold, the killer dragged one of the brothers to a cliff and kicked his body into a canyon. Then he rode from the bloody field, leaving behind three dead men, a dead dog, and another dog apparently dead.

But the dog did not die. He recovered, although one eye had been destroyed.

Sostenes was killed by his own people a few days later in an attack as violent and brutal as the one he had launched against the sheepmen. About a week later cowboys from Charles Goodnight's ranch found the dead sheepmen, their dead Navajo helper and the flock.

The flock was still together, being carefully herded by a one-eyed dog, almost dead from loss of blood and starvation.

Suggested reading: J. Evetts Haley, *Charles Goodnight, Cowman and Plainsman* (Norman: U. of Okla. Press, 1949).

STICKEEN

John Muir spent the most perilous day of his exploring career with a little black dog as his only companion. It was August, 1880, and Muir was studying glaciers in southeastern Alaska with a friend, Reverend S. H. Young, and their Indian canoe paddlers.

Muir liked dogs, but he contended that Young's small, worthless dog would only be in the way.

"This trip is not for toy dogs," Muir protested. "The poor silly thing will be in rain and snow for weeks or months, and will require care like a baby."

But Young claimed the dog could endure cold like a polar bear, swim like a seal, and had wisdom beyond human understanding. Muir looked at the short-legged, bunchy-bodied dog — about two years old — as homely as a muskrat, and wondered about his friend's judgment.

"An Irish prospector in Sitka gave him to my wife," Young said. "When we reached Fort Wrangel, the Stickeen Indians adopted him as a sort of good luck totem. That's when I named him."

At first Stickeen was aloof, as though he thought himself above the mere humans with whom he had to travel. He curled up in the bottom of a canoe, disdainfully ignoring the others. If something interesting appeared along the shore, he rested his chin on the gunwale and calmly watched. He jumped out at all stops and disappeared into the woods. He ignored the calls to hurry back when the canoes were ready to move. After the canoes were well on their way, he would trot back to the beach, jump in the water, and swim to catch up.

They tried to cure him from lagging behind by paddling farther and farther before plucking the dripping dog out of the water. But the longer the swim, the more Stickeen seemed to enjoy it.

Muir was intrigued with the dog. He tried hard to get acquainted, thinking there must be something worth while hidden beneath so much courage, endurance, and love of adventure. But Stickeen never seemed friendly. He treated Muir and the others with a haughty disdain.

On days too stormy to sail, Muir explored the woods and glaciers. Then Stickeen would follow him, wallowing through the snow and swimming ice-cold streams with the determination of an experienced mountaineer. Once he followed across a glacier so rough that every step was marked with blood. Muir stopped to wrap the dog's feet in torn strips of cloth, but Stickeen never complained.

When the party reached a large glacier in Taylor Bay, Muir planned a detailed exploration trip. The next morning a gale-force wind blew from the north, driving cold rain, laced with snow, before it in a horizontal flood, as if it were passing over the country instead of falling on it. Muir, knowing that many of nature's finest lessons are found in her storms, hurried to leave the camp. He knew the Indians and Young would stay in their tents all day, so he gave up his morning cup of coffee, hoping to get away without waking anyone. But Stickeen followed, boring his way through the icy blast.

Muir understood how a human could welcome a storm for its "exhilarating music and motion," and its opportunity to see God making landscape, But as he looked at the feeble wisp of a dog, drenched to the skin, he was bewildered. No amount of coaxing or threats would make the dog go back, so Muir turned into the storm in what he later called the most memorable of all his days.

They skirted the glacier for three miles, then climbed to its surface. Muir carved steps in the ice with his axe so the small dog could follow. At first, the crevasses were narrow or easily avoided. Some were a thousand feet deep, but whenever Muir jumped one, the little dog sailed over, oblivious to the danger of a slip. He acted as though glaciers were his playground. It took three hours to cross the glacier.

Muir explored a lake at the edge of the ice. By then it was five o'clock, and he was about fifteen miles from camp. With three hours left of storm-darkened daylight, he started back. He moved with more caution, but the dog still leaped recklessly. When he reached an eight foot-wide crevasse, Muir studied it a long time. Leaping over was no problem, but the far lip was a foot lower than the one he stood on. He knew if he went ahead, he could not come back that way. He jumped and moved on. Again, Stickeen sailed across, paying no attention to the deep gorge below.

Muir continually warned the dog to be more careful. They had been companions on previous travels, and Muir had learned to talk to him as if he were a boy and understood every word.

A few hundred yards further on, Muir reached a forty foot-wide crevasse. A narrow bridge of ice, about seventy-five feet long, ran diagonally across the gap with each end connected to the walls of the crevasse about ten feet down from the edges.

Muir carved steps down to the bridge, moved along the narrow sliver, hanging on with his knees and ankles, and carved steps up to top of the opposite edge. Never before had he been so long under such a deadly strain. He felt a great relief when he stood up. Then he wondered how he could persuade Stickeen to follow his trail. For the first time, the daring midget seemed to realize that ice was slippery and falling into a deep crevasse meant death. He stood across the gap and whined in such a human way that Muir called out to him like a child.

The stoic philosopher had become frantic, moaning and wailing as though in the bitterness of death. His emotions, so hidden before, had become transparent like the movements of a clock out of its case.

"Hush your fears, my boy. Nothing is easy in this world. We must often risk our lives to save them. At worst we can only slip, and then what a grand grave we will have!"

The despairing howls from the other side increased. Muir walked away as though leaving the dog, but Stickeen only lay down and wailed in hopeless misery. Muir returned to the edge and pleaded. He said that all he could promise was to come back and look for Stickeen the next day. If the dog went into the woods, the wolves would kill him.

Then Stickeen moved up to the edge. He slid his front feet down to the first step and appeared to be standing on his head as he slowly brought his hind feet down. He moved slowly as though taking advantage of the friction of every hair. Stickeen did that over and over until he got down to the bridge. He crossed the bridge, lifting one leg at a time as if he were concentrating on each separate step. Muir knelt to give the dog a boost as soon as he was within reach. Stickeen halted in a dead silence. He stared at each step, methodically fixing its location in his mind. Then in a rush so sudden that Muir did not see how he did it, Stickeen bounded over the top.

Muir tried to catch the dog and pet him and tell him how brave he was. But Stickeen ran and jumped and rolled over in the snow, all the time crying and screaming in "uncontrollable, exultant, triumphant joy." He made giddy loops and circles "like a leaf in a whirlwind." Muir ran up to him as he rolled in the snow, hoping to shake him out of his hysteria, as he feared he would die with joy. But the little dog flashed away for two hundred yards, his feet a mist of motion. Then he rushed back, launching himself against Muir, almost knocking him down.

The exultation lasted all the way back to camp. Stickeen flew across every crevasse. Not until dark did he slow down to his normal fox trot. They reached camp at ten o'clock and found a warm fire and a big supper. Hoonah Indians visiting Young had brought porpoise meat and wild strawberries, and Muir's hunter had brought in a wild goat. But Muir and Stickeen, too tired to eat, fell into a troubled sleep. Both of them had a fitful night, turning and twisting and moaning as they remembered crossing the crevasse.

From then on Stickeen was a changed dog. Instead of holding himself aloof, he always lay at Muir's side, keeping him constantly in sight. At night when all was quiet around the camp fire he would come to Muir and lay his head on Muir's knee as though the man were his god. Often he would catch Muir's eye as though to say, "Wasn't that an awful time we had together on the glacier?"

When the season ended, Muir returned to California. He never saw the dog again. Three years later Stickeen was stolen by a tourist at Fort Wrangel and taken away on a steamer, his fate wrapped in mystery.

As the years went on, Muir knew many dogs and had many stories to tell of their wisdom and devotion. But none ever equalled Stickeen. At first the least promising and least known of his dog-friends, he became the best known of them all. Their storm-battle for life brought the little dog to light and provided a window through which Muir looked with deeper sympathy at all his fellow mortals.

Suggested reading: John Muir, *Stickeen* (New York: Houghton Mifflin, 1909).

Globe's Dick

The stranger found time dragging heavily in the little mining camp of Globe, Arizona Territory, when he stood in front of the saloon that hot, summer afternoon. The sun burned down from the white, blinding sky and the air quivered with rising heat waves. A lonely burro a few rods away made his afternoon lunch from the contents of a litter basket, dumped into the street. Once in a while a miner slouched down the shady side of the street to disappear into a favorite saloon.

Then the stranger heard a tin can rattling, and he and the burro turned to look. The noise increased until a tiny dog came into view, an oyster can tied to his tail. A line of dust marked the trail of the terrified animal, as the can bounced and skittered behind him. He rushed on as though the can held a legion of devils.

A tall, rough-looking miner rushed out of the saloon behind the stranger, his revolver drawn. He stopped in the street, faced the oncoming dog and shouted, "Throw up your hands, Dick."

To the stranger's surprise, the little dog skidded to a stop, no longer mindful of the devil-filled can behind him. He reared up on his haunches, his little fore paws in the air and a new look on his pug face. He panted and blinked as the miner moved closer.

Then the miner grabbed Dick by the neck, holstered his weapon, and carried the dog to a bench in the shade. He began untying the can.

"Whose dog is that?" the stranger asked.

After a searching look, the miner replied. "Guess you want to buy him, no?"

"He's the best thing I've come across in the shape of a dog."

"Well, pardner, you've done hit the spike on the head. Dick is the best thing in the shape of a dog there is anywhere." He tossed the can back into the street and roughed up the dog's neck. "Say, where you from, stranger."

"Cleveland."

"I've heard of it. Back in Ohio, ain't it? Well, stranger, it would bust the biggest bank you got in Cleveland to buy this little dog. Dick belongs to Globe, he does. And you can bet your last bit of dust that Dick and Globe's going to pull together as long as Globe's Globe and Dick's Dick." He scratched the ears of the little dog, who had caught his breath and now nuzzled the leg of the miner. "Yes, sir, he's the cutinest, knowingest little beast that ever saw daylight. He's got more pluck than a bulldog." He pointed. "Jest last week he fell into that abandoned shaft over yonder. Dropped a clean, sixty-four feet he did. We was all afeared he was busted up bad. But we dropped a bucket down and hoisted him up and filled him up with beer and the next day he was like a fighting cock again."

"He drinks beer, you say?"

"That's what tickles him most. We never give him more than one glass. He'd get drunk if we let him. Course we filled him up that time he fell in the shaft."

Six weeks later the stranger was back in Globe. He and the miner recognized each other in the street.

"Back again?" The miner grabbed his hand. "Let's go have a drink."

"How's Dick?"

"Bless you. Ain't you heard? Little Dick's gone and kicked the bucket. And a sorry day it was for Globe, it was."

"What happened?"

"Well, the poor little critter hadn't had any beer for two or three days. And the durn little fool took a notion to jump back into the same shaft. He didn't fall in like before. He jist jumped straight in on purpose. Somebody saw it."

"He didn't — "

"No, he didn't land right this time. When one of the boys got to him, he just laid there on his side, whining soft and pitiful like. We hoisted him up, but he was dead when the bucket reached the top. Durn me, if it wasn't worse than if it had been one of the boys in Globe. We've had lots of men shot here without half the mourning there was for Dick."

"Did you bury him?"

"We made a little box and planted him over there on the hillside. There's a little board set up over it that says how he's Dick and he belongs to Globe and how Globe's mourning cause he's dead. It's about the first piece of hard luck Globe's had, and durn my soul it was bad enough."

Suggested reading: C. H. Buffett, "Dick, of Arizona," in *Outing* (New York, v. 10, June, 1887), 235.

FIDELITY

"It was the finest big black shepherd dog I ever saw," remembered Ranger Captain James Gillette. "These two mining engineers from Denver showed up at our camp at Ysleta. Said they were looking for a hundred pack burros. They had a new ambulance, pulled by a good team with a saddle horse tied on behind. They were prepared for Indians, too. Had shotguns, six-shooters and a nice pair of sporting rifles."

Lieutenant George Baylor suggested the men leave the Rio Grande Valley and head over to the upper Pecos to look for the animals.

"What's the best route to follow," one of them asked.

"I'd go down the stage route to Fort Davis and then follow Toyah Creek and the Pecos if it was me," Baylor said.

"That's too much out of our way. Why not take the abandoned Butterfield route past Hueco Tanks and Guadalupe Mountain?"

"Very dangerous, gentlemen. It's a hundred and fifty miles through Indian country without a white man anywhere."

The engineers, Andrews and Wiswall, headed for Hueco Tanks. On the third day, about noon, they reached Crow Flat, an abandoned station. The January wind was cold. They hobbled their horses and went inside the old shack to fry bacon and boil coffee.

A dozen Apaches slipped up on the horses so quietly even Shep, their dog, didn't hear until the thieves yelled in triumph. Andrews and Wiswall chased the Indians. Shep barked, but the Indians got away with the horses.

The miners held a council of war to decide what to do. It was one hundred miles back to Ysleta, seventy-five miles on ahead to the Pecos.

"Let's wait until dark and head back the way we came," said one.

"Shep can guard our things while we're gone," said the other.

When darkness came, they fixed two dummy sentinels to look like men on guard. They put a sack of corn and a side of bacon under their ambulance and made Shep understand that he was to guard it. Then they set out on foot.

By daybreak they had traveled twenty-five miles and were near Guadalupe Peak. They continued, taking a short cut over the mountain.

Late in the day, they crossed a ridge and saw a large band of Indians coming toward them, about two hundred yards away. The Indians yelled and started for them. Andrews and Wiswall ran up a nearby peak, threw up a breastwork of loose rocks, and opened fire.

They held the Indians off until the sun went down. Then they slipped away in the darkness. They decided to go back to Crow Flat, which they reached safely.

Shep, overjoyed to see the men, leaped up and down and barked his pleasure. The dummy sentinels were still in place, and the corn and bacon was untouched.

Andrews and Wiswall had traveled fifty miles in thirty-six hours without a wink of sleep. They slept until dark. The fifty-miles through rough country had ruined their shoes. They bound their sore and bloody feet with gunny sacks, gave Shep a new set of orders, and set out again.

Several days later, more dead than alive, the two men staggered into the ranger camp at Ysleta. Gillette left immediately with eight rangers and two mules to retrieve the ambulance left at Crow Flat.

Shep challenged the rangers as they approached on the third night. Then he seemed to recognize them as Americans and friends.

"The dog went wild with joy," Gillette said. "He barked and rolled over and over. He had eaten the side of bacon, and the corn was getting low. My men were as happy as if they had rescued a human being."

Shep had worn the top of the adobe wall around the stage station completely smooth, as he kept off the sneaking coyotes.

"We found coyote tracks all around the place," Gillette said. "But that big shepherd didn't let any of them inside the walls."

The rangers hitched their team up to the ambulance and returned to Ysleta without incident. They had traveled two hundred miles in a week.

Shep was as glad to see his masters as they were to see him.

"I don't know whether Andrews or Wiswall is still alive," Gillette wrote, "but that Mexican shepherd dog is entitled to a monument on which should be inscribed, FIDELITY."

Suggested reading: James B. Gillette, *Six Years with the Texas Rangers* (New Haven: Yale University Press, 1925).

ALL AROUND RANCH DOG

The Barker boys lived on a homestead in New Mexico. The most they could tell about their dog's ancestry was that he was half water spaniel, a quarter some kind of shepherd, an eighth bulldog of some sort, and the rest "jest dawg."

The spring 1904 runoff left Sapello Canyon meadows covered with pools of cutthroat trout. The boys enjoyed catching the trapped fish in their bare hands.

King watched the fun and decided to try it himself. His first underwater thrusts from the bank all missed. Then he learned to wade into a pool, stand quietly until the fish settled down, and grab quickly. His fish were larger than the ones the boys caught. They often kept his for eating.

The boys thought King's liking for water came from his spaniel ancestry. With his shepherd blood, he learned to chase hogs out of the corn and to drive cattle. But King became famous as the best bobcat and mountain lion dog in the territory. He never ran with trained hounds or learned by imitation. Without the help of family tradition or blue-blooded ancestry, King just "taken him a notion to tree lions — and done so." On his third hunt, he jumped four lions feeding on a deer carcass. When one lion was shot, he moved on to the next. He treed all four, one at a time.

King would eat anything from raspberries to bear meat. During haying, he bulged from eating mice, captured under hay shocks. But he feared snakes, and the boys learned to tease him about that. One would shake a hay shock, shouting, "mice." When King crouched waiting to pounce at the first wriggle in the stubble, another boy would shove a pitchfork handle between the dog's legs and shout, "snake." King would jump like a startled deer. If they pulled the joke three or four times, the insulted dog would stalk home and refuse to come out again for several hours.

King classified hunting into categories of worth. The mountain lion was the best. King would leave any deer or rabbit trail, no matter how fresh, to follow a lion trail. Bobcats were number two. Then followed deer, wild turkeys, and rabbits, with mice and chipmunks at the bottom.

King feared bears as much as snakes. Once when Omar and Marion were teen-agers, they wounded a she-bear with cubs. The wounded bear charged, and they had trouble reloading their old black powder rifle. King, although mortally afraid, stopped the bear's charge long enough for the trembling boys to get in a killing shot. The boys remembered their dog, badly hurt by the enraged bear, as an example of true courage.

Omar and Marion were out riding when one of their horses got hurt in a tangle of logs. The little mare limped so badly they stopped, treated her wound, and turned her loose. When they got home, riding double on the other horse, King was no longer with them. Three days later, they still had not seen the dog. Their father thought King had found a female companion.

When they rode out to see if the injured mare needed more treatment, they found King, gaunt and hungry, still on guard. The mare seemed alright, so they called the dog and headed for home. King still refused to come. He sat by the mare, a forlorn look on his face, and refused to budge. So they caught the mare and led her home. King trotted happily at her heels.

One day, one of the Barker's saddle mares was brought in from the high country with a mule foal at her side. The boys named the little colt, Macho. Macho thought King was a coyote. He laid his ears back and charged, stomping with his small, hard feet. King yelped and ran while Macho brayed humiliating mule laughter. The dog recovered his dignity and rushed the surprised mule, nipping at his heels. Macho limped away with his mother.

The feud, playful but tinged with hatefulness, lasted all summer and fall. That winter, Macho's mother was killed by a mountain lion. When the ranch ponies were caught up in the spring, Macho was so weak he could not renew the feud until after a few weeks of grazing in the meadow.

The spring Macho was three, the Barkers decided to leave him in the high country. When the foreman rode out for the spare ponies, King picked up a lion trail and ran ahead. The foreman heard the lion snarling, King barking, and Macho braying as he hurried on up the trail. He found the lion dead, his neck chewed to a pulp, his hind legs and hips broken and crushed. Nearby a badly injured King was licking the wounds of an equally injured Macho. The mule followed the foreman back to the ranch and never left it again.

The feud between King and Macho was over. They had conquered a lion together.

Suggested reading: Fairfax Downey, *Great Dog Stories of all Time* (Garden City: Doubleday & Co., 1962).

MOUNTAIN CLIMBER

Enos A. Mills, the father of Rocky Mountain National Park, climbed Long's Peak 250 times. A memorable ascent for him was one he did not make; he sent his collie, Scotch, to take his place.

Mills got Scotch as a puppy. The dog grew tall and athletic. Scotch enjoyed his excursions into the woods from Mills' cabin on Long's Peak. He barked at all strangers. He enjoyed Mills' other pets, showing some reserve toward the grizzly cub.

Scotch learned to recognize several words. If Mills said "hatchet," the dog would bring it. When Mills said "fire," Scotch would search for flames and bark when he found them.

Scotch showed remarkable intelligence. A neighborhood pack of coyotes once teased him with a decoy. That night was the first time Scotch stayed out all night. The next day he returned with another collie who lived at a ranch fifteen miles down the mountain. Scotch seemed worried until Mills welcomed the stranger. Mills was impressed with the collies' teamwork when the coyotes returned. The visiting collie hid, and Scotch walked forward into view. The dogs trapped the decoy and soundly whipped it. The coyote pack never tried that trick again. Mills learned later from the tracks in the trail that Scotch had walked the visiting collie part way home.

Scotch enjoyed playing ball. He and Mills would toss a ball back and forth, keeping it in the air for many turns. The dog even learned to keep the ball in the air, himself.

Scotch had a natural dignity. He disdained people trying to teach him to jump over a stick, sit up and beg, or roll over and play dead. He loved hide and seek, and he played with the same imagination demonstrated by children. Mills would pretend to search for Scotch. The dog, crouching nearby in plain view, pretended to be hidden. Mills would approach him from different directions, saying, "Where is Scotch? Where is Scotch?" The dog, too happy to bark, would hug the earth, silently. Sometimes he pretended to be looking at something in the distance. From time to time, when Mills' back was turned, Scotch would stealthily move to a new "hiding" place. Not until Mills cried, "Oh, there's Scotch," would the game be over. Then the dog would yelp in ecstacy, leaping into his master's arms.

45

ENOS MILLS AND SCOTCH
Denver Public Library
Western History Department

In 1906 Victoria Broughm, a young woman from Michigan, wanted to climb Long's Peak without a guide. Mills agreed, provided she took Scotch with her. As the woman started her climb, Mills charged the dog: "Scotch, go with this young woman up Long's Peak. Keep her on the trail. Take good care of her, and stay with her until she returns." Scotch barked and started up the trail. He switched his tail smartly from side to side, as though impressed with Mills' confidence and his own responsibility.

The young woman climbed steadily to timberline. Then she took a long rest to enjoy the brilliant alpine flowers in the September sunshine. She reached the peak in late afternoon, and again she rested to enjoy the beauty and grandeur. Soon after she started down, the sky turned cloudy and dark. She missed the cairns that marked the trail and started down the deep and rugged Glacier Gorge.

Until then, Scotch had minded his own affairs, enjoying himself on the mountain. Now he sprang forward, taking the lead aggressively. The woman thought he was tired and trying to run away. She refused to follow him. She continued on the wrong trail. Scotch planted himself in front of her and refused to budge. She scolded him harshly and reminded him that his master had told him to take care of her. She continued on the wrong trail. Scotch followed meekly behind. He had tried to do his first task; now he would do the second.

The two spent the night in 100-mile-an-hour winds at 13,000 feet. The woman lay down behind some rocks and hugged Scotch closely to stay warm. Mills' rescue party found the pair at sunrise. The woman was exhausted. Her lips were blue and cracked, but only her fingers were frostbitten. At first she was unable to walk, but with the help of the rescuers, she started slowly down the mountain. When Scotch saw the rescuers approach, he knew he was discharged from his duty. He ran home for breakfast.

Victoria Broughm was the first woman to climb a major Colorado peak alone. But she never described it that way. She always mentioned Scotch, sure that her companion had saved her life.

Suggested reading: Enos A. Mills, *The Story of Scotch* (Boston: Houghton Mifflin, 1935).

A MESSAGE LEARNED

The importance of good dogs on the frontier is illustrated by an incident in Abilene, Kansas, in late October, 1879. Some strangers were admiring the dog of a Mister Smith, when one of them offered a hundred dollars for the animal.

"He's worth more than that to me," Smith said, declining the offer.

Wichita Tom, a fancy dressing gambler loafing nearby, overheard the conversation. He strolled over, drew his pistol, and said, "I'll bring the value of that brute right down to the market."

Before the astonished witnesses could act, Tom shot the dog through the jaw, knocking out four teeth and permanently mutilating the animal. The indignant witnesses overpowered the assailant and turned him over to the city marshal. When they learned that the only charge that could be filed was shooting a gun within the city limits, Abilene citizens began making their own plans.

Wichita Tom's protection in the jail ended at three the next morning. About fifty Abilene citizens took the man, now begging for his life, to a railroad trestle, threw a rope over a beam, and strung him up. One of them held a watch. At the end of exactly three minutes, they let the man down.

"You got more life in you than we figured on," one of them said. "I guess we'll have to hoist you up again."

This time Wichita Tom hung for exactly one minute, but it was enough to make him lose consciousness.

After the citizens revived him and untied the rope, one of them announced: "We're giving you a reprieve, Wichita Tom. It will come to an end the next time we see you."

Tom got the message and left town without delay. He never returned.

Suggested reading: How they Handle Dog Fiends in Kansas, in *Forest and Stream* (New York, v. 13, November 13, 1879), p. 807.

CRIME-SOLVER

About sundown on December 5, 1916, the stage from Rogerson, Idaho, was three hours overdue at Jarbridge, Nevada. Postmaster Scott Fleming knew that four thousand dollars in cash was coming in the mail, so he sent Frank Leonard into a raging blizzard to look for the stage. Two nights before, wagons meeting on the narrow trail into Jarbridge had taken all night to get past each other. Fleming was afraid the stage had slipped off the trail in the storm, falling to the bottom of the canyon.

When Leonard returned without seeing anything, a search party went back into the snowstorm for a closer look. They found the stage only a quarter mile from town. Driver Fred Searcy, a bullet hole in the back of his head, lay sprawled over the seat, his body glued fast by frozen blood. The horses were tied to a willow clump near the river. Blood-smeared contents from the second class mail sack lay scattered in the snow. The first class sack with its cash was gone.

The rising fury of the storm drove the searchers back to their little town in the bottom of a narrow canyon. They all had the unsettling thought that the killer was surely still in their midst.

When the searchers went back out after daylight, they found tracks of a man and a dog. J. B. McCormick, mercantile store owner and an experienced hunter, blew the fresh, light snow out of one of the tracks and discovered a print in the older snow beneath. He knew the dog was a large one.

There weren't many large dogs in the town, and McCormick decided to watch them closely.

"Who knows," he said, "maybe the dog'll show up and lead us to the killer."

About ten o'clock that morning, McCormick and others saw a large, yellow mongrel sniffing along the fresh-fallen snow, as though following a trail. Suddenly the dog bounded into the willows and started pawing the snow. The onlookers saw him uncover the first class mail sack. It held blood-smeared letters, but the money was gone.

To no one's surprise, the dog's paws matched the prints near the scene of the crime.

"Who's dog is it?" McCormick asked.

"He runs in that pack that don't really belong to no one," said one. "They're just tramp dogs."

"But he likes to follow Ben Kuhl around," said another.

BEN KUHL

Nevada Historical Society

"That part-time cook that's on bond for jumping a claim?"

"Yeah. He's done time in California and Oregon, too."

"He's a mean son of a bitch. That dog's about the only friend he's got."

Further search turned up a bloody shirt and coat. The coat had hung in a cabin which Kuhl shared with two others. Search of the cabin produced a recently-fired revolver which was also tied to Kuhl.

Kuhl pleaded guilty for a life sentence. He was paroled in 1945. One report says he died in San Francisco a year later. Another says he was hitchhiking back to Jarbridge from his parole release when he was killed by a hit and run driver. The four thousand dollars has never been found.

The Jarbridge murder and trial were notable in two respects. The hold-up was the last one in this country of a horse-drawn stage. The trial was the first one in which identification evidence from a palm print was admitted into a trial. Kuhl's bloody palm print had been found on one of the envelopes.

The case may also be one of the clearest where the behavior of a dog helped solve a crime.

Suggested reading: Helen E. Wilson, *Gold Fever* (La Mesa, CA: Privately printed, 1974).

SWITCH ENGINE BRUNO

No one knew his origin. Some thought his mother had been herding sheep in the mountains of southwestern Montana. But yellow staghounds were not common in sheep camps. Others thought he was a derelict. He was just a puppy when he showed up in Bozeman in 1924.

"Maybe his master got killed or took sick and died," said some.

"Don't look much like a ranch dog," observed others. "Hard to tell where he could be from."

No one remembers who named him Bruno, but much of the world learned of his love affair with engine 911 of the Northern Pacific Railroad.

Dogs have adopted rabbits, Guinea pigs, chickens, horses, mules, goats, and a host of other animals, but Bruno is the only one known to have adopted a switch engine. When the railroaders in the Bozeman yards first saw him, they tried to chase him away for his own good. Railroad yards with their many tracks and all kinds of trains running back and forth are not safe places for puppies.

But something attracted Bruno to old 911. He dodged the railroaders' menacing sticks and thrown ballast, ignored their threats, and kept his eye on his new love, his tail wagging constantly.

When 911 rolled forward, Bruno followed; when it moved backward, he still followed. When it stopped he lay down nearby, his eyes alert, his ears cocked, awaiting the release of air that signalled the locomotive's imminent movement.

He learned to watch the switchman to learn which direction his pal would go. Then he darted ahead or backward, leading the way. Well-worn trails padded into the cinder ballast began to mark the most common routes for 911 in its daily yard work. Bruno had no interest in people or other dogs. His entire life centered on the switch engine.

Keeping up with 911 was hard work. Bruno learned to time his mealtimes with those of the yard crew. When they ate, he ate. When they worked overtime, he worked overtime. Many days the engine would travel sixty miles, its faithful companion keeping it company the whole distance. When the engine ran into the roundhouse to retire for the night, Bruno would follow, happy to finally get some rest beside his true love.

Bruno even learned to carry a stick in his mouth, copying the switchman with his break club.

For five years Bruno and old 911 were inseparable. The railroaders in the yards and the station as well as the crews of through trains came to expect him whenever 911 moved. Then one day — no one knows how — the strange marriage ended in tragedy.

Perhaps Bruno was tired or his stick was too heavy. Perhaps the engineer or the switchman was careless. But old 911 ran over and crushed its faithful partner.

The grief-stricken yard crewmen, who had once tried to chase Bruno away, buried his remains in the east end of the yards. They took up a collection and bought a marker for the grave.

Newspaper readers from New York to the West Coast read all about the strange pairing of the yellow staghound and the switch engine. Tourists passing through Bozeman would leave their trains long enough to pay respects at Bruno's grave marker.

About fifty years later Burlington Northern, successor to the Northern Pacific, closed its station in Bozeman. Railroad employees who still treasured the story of Bruno rescued the grave marker and had it moved to safety. It can now be seen in the front yard of the Park County Museum in nearby Livingston, Montana.

Suggested reading: Newspaper clippings in Park County Museum, Livingston, Montana.

SWITCH ENGINE BRUNO'S GRAVE MARKER

Livingston, Montana

FETCH ON THE RAILROAD

Many dogs enjoy retrieving objects thrown by their masters. For Jack, a shepherd who struggled one day into the Santa Fe railroad station at Peach Springs, Arizona, the game was particularly exciting. It almost put him in the movies.

Jack came into the station on a summer evening, exhausted. His bleeding paws and dust-caked coat showed that he had dragged himself across many miles of northern Arizona desert. The station agent, A. M. Browning, bandaged the dog's paws, fed him, and gave him his name. No one ever claimed him.

A month passed before Jack could walk without limping. Then Browning began teaching the dog. Jack learned to keep stray burros, dogs and horses away from the station. But his favorite sport was retrieving order hoops, thrown by his master.

An order hoop was a lightweight loop with a wooden handle, into which train orders were stuffed. When a train came through a station without stopping, the station agent used order hoops to pass along the crew's orders for the next section of the line. He would stand on the platform as the train passed through, holding the hoop up so a crewman on the train could grab it on the fly. Most trains required two hoops, one for the engine crew in front and one for the conductor at the rear. Double headers, with additional engines at the rear, might require a third hoop.

After the crew member pulled the orders out, he would toss the hoop back so the station agent could recover it to use again. With some trains going forty miles an hour, it often took considerable time to retrieve the hoops. Jack's favorite game saved his master many miles of walking in the desert.

Browning died, and the new agent gave Jack to a state policeman. By then, though, Jack had railroad blood in his veins, and he refused to stay with his new master. Every morning when the new agent, H. W. Hutchinson, opened the station, Jack was waiting at the door. He continued to retrieve the order hoops, and Hutchinson decided to keep him.

Sometimes, to tease Jack, Hutchinson would get out the order hoops but remain in his chair as he heard the train approaching. Then Jack would frantically run to the door, look out, run to the order hoops on the counter, and then to his master to remind him of his duty. If Hutchinson still didn't move, Jack would prod his master until he picked up the hoops.

Sometimes it took as long as thirty minutes for Jack to find an order hoop which had fallen in thick weeds. But he never failed to bring them in. On rare occasions a hoop would land under the train and be broken. Then Jack would bring it in one piece at a time.

Once, when a slow freight passed through, Jack retrieved the head-end hoop before the conductor got the rear-end hoop. Then Jack ran to the rear of the train, waiting for the conductor to throw back his hoop. But the conductor sat down on the caboose platform and read his orders, holding the hoop in his hand. Jack bounded along, keeping pace with the train, frustrated that the conductor didn't do his part. Finally he made a huge leap, grabbing the hoop with his teeth and jerking it out of the conductor's hand. He ran back to the station in triumph.

The baggageman on Train No. 8 threw off a small roll of newspapers every morning. Jack also learned to catch those and bring them into the station. One morning he was so intent on catching the roll that he did not notice a local train coming in on the other track. As he whirled to catch the bundle, he was hit a glancing blow by a journal box on the other train. He was not hurt seriously, but he wobbled for several days as he continued chasing hoops.

Jack's reputation grew. Two Hollywood scouts came to Peach Springs with offers to buy him. Hutchinson, realizing that leaving the railroad would break Jack's heart, refused to sell.

One day Jack limped home with a bullet in his side. He died a few minutes after reaching the station. Santa Fe railroaders tried for months to locate the killer. They made inquiries from Seligman to Kingman, but learned nothing.

They buried Jack near the tracks at Peach Springs. They hoped that Jack, in some far away place beyond the Big Rock Candy Mountain, would still hear the train whistles and dash away after his beloved order hoops.

Suggested reading: Freeman H. Hubbard, *Railroad Avenue* (New York: McGraw Hill Book Co., Inc., 1945).

BEWILDERED KING

An express agent in an Arizona village received a crated collie puppy, shipped to George Rogers. Rogers refused to accept the animal. The agent fed the puppy a few weeks and then turned him loose to fend for himself.

"Too bad, Jack," the agent said, "Nobody wants you, and I can't take care of you any longer."

Enos Mills, visiting in the village that summer, noticed the puppy. He seemed to have some inherited memories associated with sheep. He would stand and watch sheep as though he realized he was supposed to do something but did not know what it was.

Mills returned to the village two years later. Jack was still there. Mills noticed then that the collie also stood and watched goats, as though ready to take charge of the herd. He seemed to be thinking that something ought to be done. But no one ever told him what it was.

Jack grew up in a lonely world, without responsibility. No one reached out a friendly hand or called with a friendly voice. The dog often wandered away at night, sometimes for fifteen or twenty miles. He was easy to notice; he was the only Collie in the area. No one ever searched for him or tried to bring him back.

Then Jack met a woman who came to the village and built a house on the mountain. She was pleased that the dog followed her. He did not want to be petted, but he liked to follow the woman, making sure no one harmed her. She fed him, and each time he seemed surprised that food came from a human hand.

The woman, a Mrs. Helms, moved to another town. She took Jack with her. Then she went back East for an extended visit. She turned Jack over to a neighbor, but the neighbor died, and Jack was again homeless and alone.

By the time Mrs. Helms returned, Jack had joined a pack of coyotes. The wild animals accepted him as their leader. He took one of the females as his mate.   Some time after that, Mills again saw Jack. At that time, Mills was studying plants and geology near the Grand Canyon. Cowboys from nearby ranches told Mills they had seen the dog several times. They, too, noticed his peculiar behavior around cattle, particularly calves. They told Mills the dog seemed to want more than the carefree life of a coyote. He needed to be active, doing something important.

A cowboy said he had seen Jack when a coyote and a dog come upon a group of stray calves. The collie walked among the calves as though he were personally interested in them, but did not know what he was supposed to do. His coyote mate looked at him, puzzled. Jack, too, was puzzled. He seemed to be thinking: "Here are stray calves. It seems to me I ought to do something with them, but what is it I'm supposed to do?" Finally, Jack lay down and watched the calves a long time. At last he slunk away, as though he knew he had shirked a duty. He looked back over his shoulder several times. Once he seemed close to returning and resuming his guard.

One time Jack and his mate came upon a band of sheep. Jack, excited, ran toward the herder, while the coyote skulked nearby. The herder thought it was a coyote trick to stampede his flock, and he fired his rifle at Jack. The baffled dog turned and ran back to his mate.

Jack became a legend among the prospectors and ranchers on the Arizona desert. They called him the King of the Coyotes. Many times they heard among coyote calls a deeper sound. Neither a bark nor a howl, it spoke of mystery and loneliness.

When Mrs. Helms returned from the East and saw that Jack was gone, she searched for him. She went to the town where she had lived earlier and had first seen the dog. She learned more about Jack's interest in cattle and sheep, but she could not find him.

But Jack found her. He returned to the place where she had left him with the neighbor. Mrs. Helms, now living there again, was delighted to find him. She took him out to a sheep ranch for a few days. Jack seemed happy at having something to do. He quickly learned to handle sheep. He was glad to finally have some responsibility. Mrs. Helms could see his enjoyment, and she, too, was happy. She bought her own sheep ranch so Jack would have work he enjoyed.

She bought the ranch from the express agent in the town where she had formerly lived. Then she learned for the first time that Jack was the little collie she had shipped west for her son.

Suggested reading: Enos A. Mills, *Waiting in the Wilderness* (Garden City: Doubleday Page, 1921).

WHAT A DOG, WHAT A MAN

Jim Forbes of Forbes Landing, British Columbia, was reminiscing about cougar hunting on Vancouver Island in the 1920s.

"Is it dangerous?" he was asked.

"Naw. Track 'em with dogs. Chase 'em up a tree and shoot. Nothing to it. Cougars are cowards."

"No adventure to it?"

"Not for me. But I had a dog once that sure had some troubles with it. If you want, I could tell you."

"Go ahead. I always like to hear about dogs."

"His name was Buster. It was February, 1926. We were hunting near Buttle's Lake when Buster picked up the trail of this cripple."

Jim looked into the fireplace. "Guess I should start at the beginning, which was three years before. You see, some trappers had got oiled up over Christmas and didn't tend their traps right. They had caught a cougar by the right front paw and he chewed his own leg apart and got away. I come across his tracks from time to time during the next three years."

"So he was a three-legged lion?"

"Right."

"What happened in twenty-six?"

"Well, we ran him down to the lake shore and he tried to climb a tree, but couldn't make the grade with just the one front paw. He fell back three times with Buster nipping at him. He tried again to get up the tree each time he fell back. The fourth time was sort of a clinch. They rolled over and over down a snowdrift with fur flying like crazy. I didn't dare shoot for fear of hitting Buster. Then they skittered out on the ice and dropped into the water.

"The big cat was snarling something terrible, but you couldn't hear a sound from Buster. He was just a mongrel — Irish terrier and collie — but he knew where he had the advantage, so he kept trying to pull the cougar under. Once, when they were turning over slowly, I got a shot into the cougar's neck, which finished him. But he let out a dying scream and then closed his teeth down on Buster's left leg, breaking every bone in the joint above his paw."

Jim licked the end of a cigar, took his time in lighting it, and continued. "Buster dragged the cougar into shallow water and came limping up to me. I could see right away that

that dying, three-legged cougar had handed me back a three-legged dog. I went sick to my stomach seeing it; I loved that dog so much. I got him bandaged up and into my boat and traveled twenty miles by water, not even stopping for lunch."

"Alone?"

"Just me and Buster. On the second day we got to the end of water, so I made up a light pack, wrapped Buster in my coat, and carried him three days on my back over the mountain. We only stopped to camp and wash Buster's leg. On the third day, while he was licking his wound, some little bones fell out. Not once, on the whole trip did he ever whine or complain. He would just look up at me while I was feeding him or washing the wound and wag his tail."

"What did the pack weigh, counting the dog?"

"About seventy-five pounds. We had snow all the way. Every night I took him under my blankets, so I could keep him warm. He would lick my face, knowing what a fix he was in and trusting me to get him home some way or other. The last few days, I rigged up a toboggan and took the hill into Forbes Landing. Lucky it was down hill or I never would have made it."

"Was there a doctor there?"

"No, but we reached Campbell River Station the next day. I sent Buster on from there to Vancouver. He was six weeks in the hospital and came back a raring to go cougar hunting again."

"Did he get any more?"

"We killed ten more that season before the snow went out. But he was always leaving a blood trail in the snow. You see, the stump would bleed from bumping against something or hitting ice splinters. It was too much like trailing the three-legged cougar, and I couldn't keep doing it."

"What did you do?"

"I took Buster off the mountains and made him stay around the landing. He lived three more years and was just like a member of my family."

Jim pointed. "There on the wall is his picture. He was just a mongrel, but what a dog. What a dog!"

Suggested reading: Robert H. Davis, *The More I Admire Dogs* (New York: D. Appleton-Century Co., 1936).

FAITHFUL FRIEND

In August, 1936, the body of Tony, a sheepherder, was brought to Fort Benton, Montana, for shipment east on the Great Northern Railroad. The man's nondescript dog, mostly collie, watched with questioning eyes as the trainmen loaded the coffin. Shep knew that his master was inside the box, and he did not understand. He whined when the engine whistled and the train moved slowly out of the station. Then he turned and trotted away, his head hanging low that his master had left him there, alone.

When the next train pulled into the station, Shep returned to the platform, hoping that his master had come back. He watched expectantly as train crew and passengers moved about. But neither the box nor the master came off the train. Busy with their work and travel, no one had a friendly word or pat for the forlorn dog. Shep's tail, wagging with hope when the train pulled in, drooped in sadness as it pulled out. Shep was back for the next train and the next and the next and the one after that.

Station Agent A. V. Schanche noticed that Shep had made a place for himself in a cool corner under the platform. Now and then the agent coaxed him out for a few scraps of food. But Shep grew gaunt as summer days turned to fall and then the winds and snow of winter blew in.

Shep still met every train from both directions. People began to talk about the faithful dog. The diner crews left choice scraps for agent Schanche to feed. Pat McSweeney, section foreman, tried to move Shep into the section house. But the dog refused to leave the spot where he had last seen his master.

All through 1937 and 1938, Shep met every train. He looked intently at every arriving passenger and he examined every large box, handed off by baggagemen. As each train pulled out, he returned wearily and dejected to his place under the platform, to lie and wait for the whistle of the next train.

From time to time sheepmen came down from the hills to see if they could take Shep to their wagons and give the faithful dog a new home. But Shep did not want new friends. He just wanted to get back with the best friend he had ever had. The station agent also tried to bring Shep inside, particularly in the winters. But the dog refused to be shut up in a place where he might not be able to greet his master when he returned.

For ten days in Spring 1939, Shep disappeared. But those were days when trains could not run through Fort Benton. Warm chinook winds had melted snow to wash out some of the track. When the first train came back, Shep again appeared on the platform to continue his vigil.

The nation began to notice as Shep's story was told in many places, both in the United States and abroad. Pastors used Shep's faithfulness as sermon topics. Robert Ripley featured the dog in Believe it or Not. Letters poured in from over the world, and Shep was called the most popular dog in America. So many letters came that the division superintendent appointed his secretary to handle the mail. The countless offers of new homes were politely declined. It was obvious that Shep wanted to meet each train, making sure that his master did not return without a proper greeting from his faithful friend.

So Shep continued meeting trains in 1939 and all through 1940 and 1941. Even though the nation was becoming more and more involved in a growing war, people still traveled to Fort Benton, just to see the faithful dog. Shep didn't mind the crowds; there were just more people to check out in his search for the master. But he was a one-man dog, and he resented the attempts to pet him, and even to take pictures. Finally, the very sight of a camera would send him running.

On January 12, 1942, Great Northern Train No. 235 pulled in to the Fort Benton station. When Shep heard the whistle, he came out on the platform and stepped on to the tracks to watch the train approach. Over five years of waiting in all kinds of weather had taken its toll. Shep's eyes had dimmed and his ears had muffled. The tracks were slick with snow. Shep slipped, and the train ran over him before it could stop. Shep could finally join his master.

The mayors of Great Falls and Fort Benton led the funeral procession to the top of a nearby hill. The pastor from the Fort Benton Christian Church preached the sermon. Boy Scouts of Troop 47 were pall bearers, and the troop bugler sounded taps.

Afterward, Great Northern employees built a concrete monument to Shep. The railroad installed a spotlight so passengers on night trains could see it as they passed through. It was a fitting tribute to the most faithful of man's faithful friends.

Suggested reading: *The Story of Shep* (Fort Benton: The River Press).

ORDERING INFORMATION

True Tales of the Old West is projected for 36 volumes.

Proposed titles include:

Warriors and Chiefs	In print
Soldiers	In print
Native Women	In print
Mountain Men	In print
Pioneer Women	In print
Ranchers and Cowboys	In print
Horses and Riders	In print
Miners	In print
Entertainers	In print
Dogs and Masters	In print
Outlaws	In print
Frontiersmen	In print
Lawmen	Soon to appear
Gamblers	Soon to appear
Homesteaders	Soon to appear
Explorers	Under way
Lawyers & Judges	Under way
Scouts	Under way
Writers	Under way
Railroaders	Started
Merchants	Started
Army Women	Started
Vigilantes	Started

Ask at your bookstore or write:

PIONEER PRESS
Box 216
Carson City, NV 89702-0216